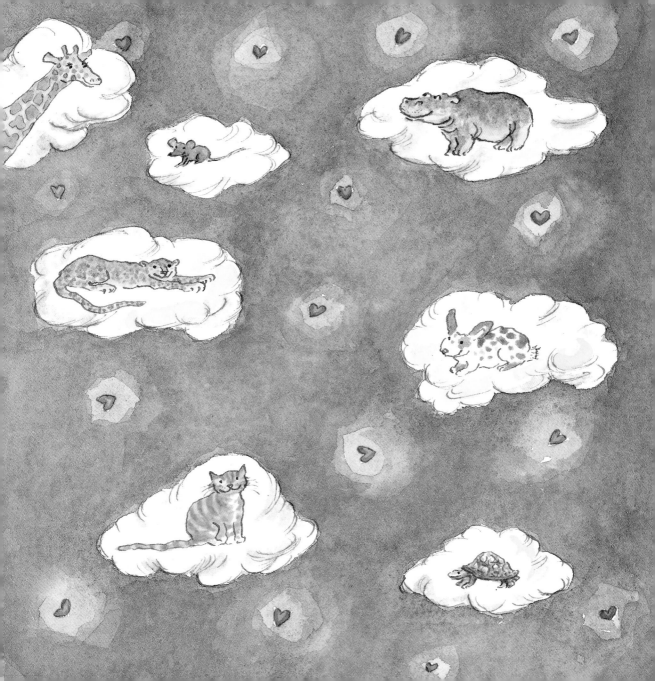

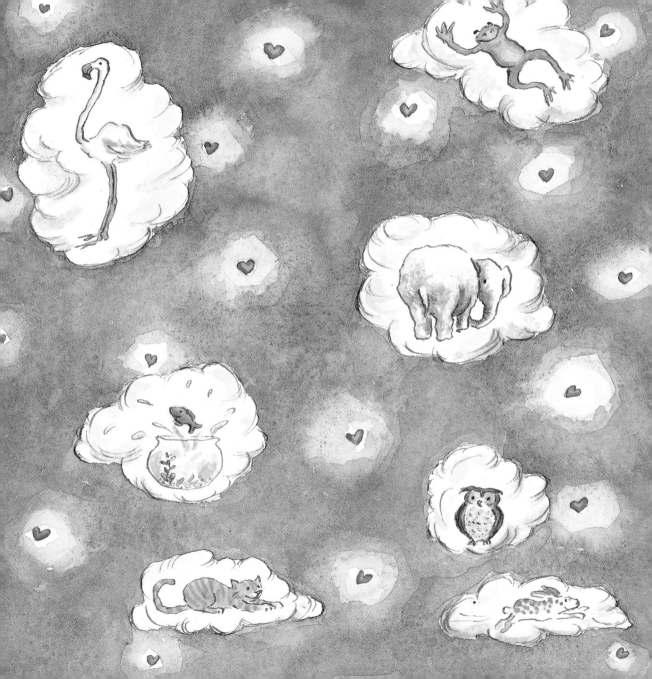

for
Jerry & Anne

Boots & Pandora

First published in Great Britain by HarperCollins Publishers Ltd in 1995.
ISBN 0 00 761365 2 Text and illustrations copyright © Rachel Pank 1995.
Printed and bound in Singapore. This book is set in Educational Garamond 24/30.

My Perfect Pet

Rachel Pank

Collins
A Division of HarperCollinsPublishers

Some pets are very large
Some are rather small,

Some like lots of water

And others none at all.

A rabbit runs too fast

A tortoise goes too slow,

A giraffe stands too high

And a mouse creeps too low.

Some pets grow too fat

Some are much too thin,

Some won't play outside

And others won't
come in.

My dog Bill's the perfect pet

I would not have another.

Except, of course,
for my dog Ben,
His identical
twin brother!

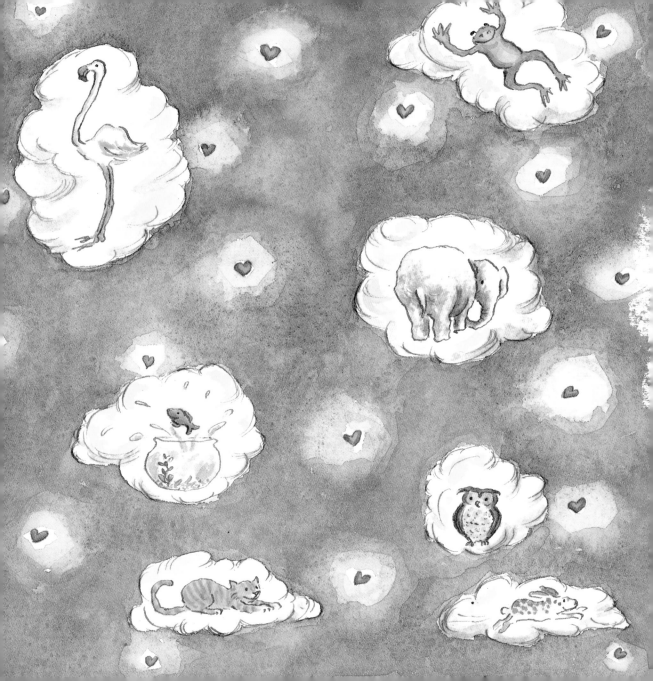